Bed Hogs

By **Kelly DiPucchio** ✳ Illustrated by **Howard Fine**

Hyperion Books for Children / New York

With special thanks to Steven Malk, Donna Bray, Lisa Wheeler, and Hope Vestergaard — K.D.

Text copyright © 2004 by Kelly DiPucchio ◆ Illustrations copyright © 2004 by Howard Fine
For information address Hyperion Books for Children, 114 Fifth Avenue, New York, New York 10011-5690.

Printed in Hong Kong

First Edition

1 3 5 7 9 10 8 6 4 2

This book is set in 20-point Lemonade Bold.

Reinforced binding

ISBN 0-7868-1884-0

Library of Congress Cataloging-in-Publication Data on file.

Visit www.hyperionbooksforchildren.com.

To Laurel, Nicholas, and Hannah, the original bed hogs—with love.
And to John, who makes life much better — K.D.

To Nate, on the occasion of his birth — H.F.

In Sooey, South Dakota,
in a sloppy, stuffy sty,
there's an itchy ol' straw bed
where the Bed Hogs pile high.

'Course, the mama and the papa
take up lots of space in bed,
but so do sisters Rose and Flo,
and big, blue-ribbon Ed.

Each night the hogs pack into bed—
they squeeze and groan and grunt.
But underneath the ton of them
squeals loudmouth Little Runt.

"I'm squished!
    I'm squashed!
        I'm buried in this heap!
You're hoggin' up my space in bed.
I'll *never* get to sleep!"

Rose, the reigning beauty queen,
is tender, pink, and sweet.
But more than just a pretty face—
Rose has some stinky feet!

Runt gave sweet Rose a little shove.

She tumbled out of bed.

That left **5** hogs in the pile—

Runt snuggled in and said . . .

Big sister Flo's a tidy hog,
groomed neat from head to tail,
but late at night she drools enough
to fill a milkin' pail.

Runt gave big Flo a little push.

She slipped right out of bed.

That left **4** hogs in the pile—

Runt snuggled in and said . . .

Brother Ed is quite a ham—
his jokes give *him* the giggles.
But when he has a funny dream
the hog bed shakes and jiggles.

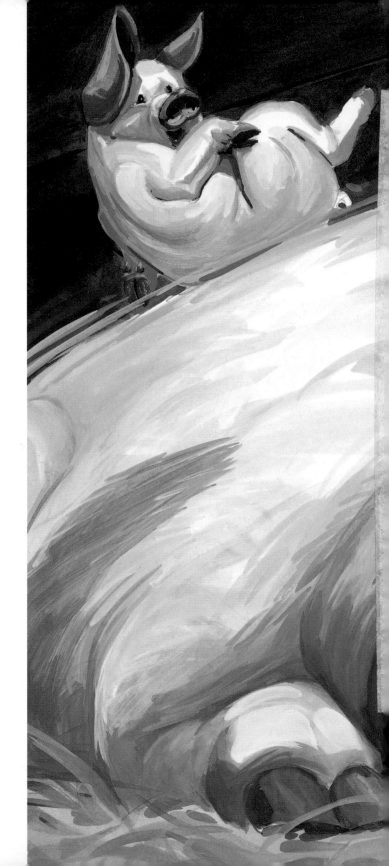

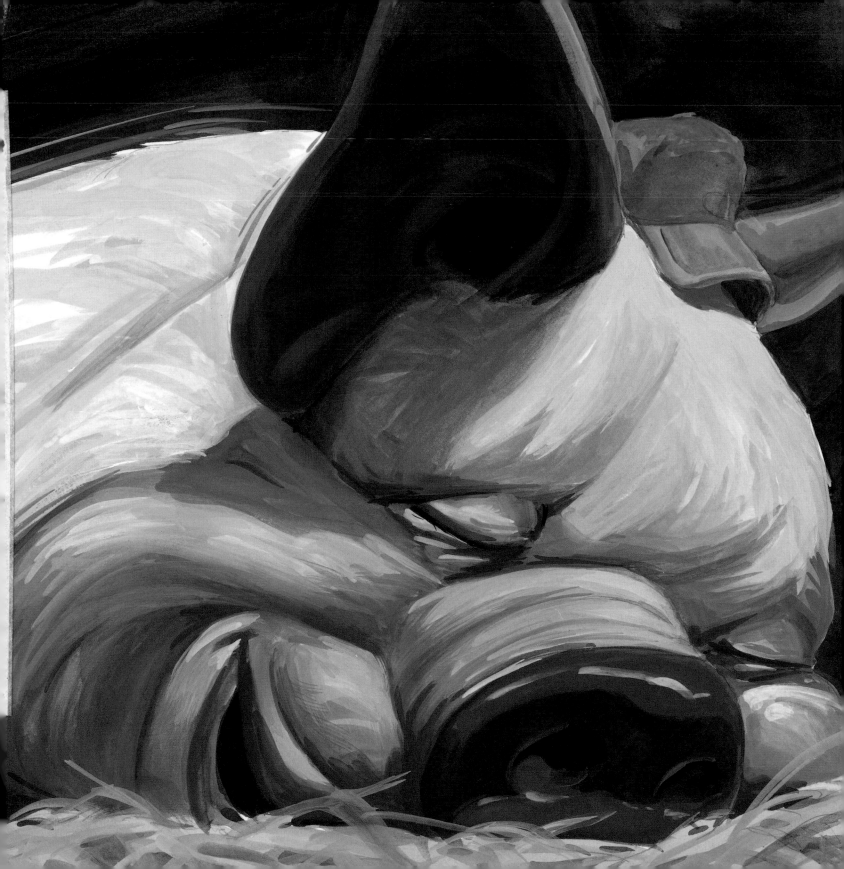

Runt tickled Ed behind the ear.
Ed laughed right out of bed.

That left **3** hogs in the pile—
Runt snuggled in and said . . .

Mama dances in her sleep—
she spins and twirls and hops.
But all that fancy footwork
means a swift kick in the chops.

"Ouch!"

Runt swung his mama round and round.
She two-stepped off the bed.

That left **2** hogs in the pile—
Runt snuggled in and said . . .

Papa hardly moves at all,
he's still as fleas in muck,
but from his snout there comes a snore
that rumbles like a truck.

"Shhh!"

Runt sprinkled fresh black
pepper into Papa's noisy snout.
That sneezing really did the trick,
'cause Papa Hog fell out!

Now there was **1** hog in the bed . . .

. . . just one sleepyhead.

No Mama.
No Papa.
No sisters.
No Ed!

Runt hunkered down beneath the straw,
alone there in the stack.
He closed his eyes and hollered loud . . .

"I'm cold!
      I'm scared!
            I'm lonely in this heap!
Without y'all hoggin' up the bed,
I'll *never* get to sleep!"

So all the hogs came runnin'
and hopped back into bed:
Mama, Papa, Rose, and Flo,
and big, blue-ribbon Ed.

In Sooey, South Dakota,
on an itchy ol' straw bed,
the Bed Hogs piled high again—
Runt snuggled in and said . . .

"Ahhhhh, much better!"

Zzz End!